Jingle-Jingle

Nicola Smee

Boxer Books

"Who wants a ride
in my sleigh?"
asks Mr. Horse.

"We do, please, Mr. Horse,"
say Cat
and Dog
and Pig
and Duck.

"Hold on tight!"
says Mr. Horse.
And off they go...

Jingle-jingle!

Jingle-jingle!

"Let's go over the fields,"
say Cat and Dog
and Pig and Duck.

"Very well," says Mr. Horse. "But hold on TIGHT!"

And off they go...

Jingle-jingle, crunch-crunch.

Jingle-jingle, crunch-crunch.

"Can we slide
down the hill,
please, Mr. Horse?"
ask Cat and Dog
and Pig and Duck.

"Very well,"
says Mr. Horse.
"Is there room for me?"

"Of course, Mr. Horse,
but make sure you
hold on TIGHT!"
say Cat
and Dog
and Pig
and Duck.

And off they go...

Jingle-jingle,
swoosh-swoosh!
Faster, faster,
goes the sleigh.
Jingle-jingle,
swoosh-swoosh!

Faster, faster, goes the sleigh!

Look out!
Look out!

Jingle-plop! Jingle-plop! Jingle-plop-plop-plop!

Cat and Dog and Pig and Duck land in the cold and crunchy snow...

and so does Mr. Horse!

"Oh dear! Oh dear!
Oh dearie me!"

cry Cat
and Dog
and Pig
and Duck.

"That was SO COOL!"

says happy Mr. Horse.

"Come on, then, Mr. Horse!"
say Cat and Dog
and Pig and Duck.

And off they all go again.
Jingle-jingle, swoosh-swoosh!

W h e e e

eeeeee!

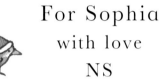

For Sophia
with love
NS

First American edition published in 2008
by Boxer Books Limited.

Distributed in the United States and Canada by
Sterling Publishing Co., Inc.
387 Park Avenue South, New York, NY 10016-8810

First published in Great Britain in 2008
by Boxer Books Limited.
www.boxerbooks.com

ISBN 13: 978-1-906250-08-9
ISBN 10: 1-906250-08-1

Printed in China

All of our papers are sourced from managed forests and renewable resources.

PKD1372